Just Grace and the Snack Attack

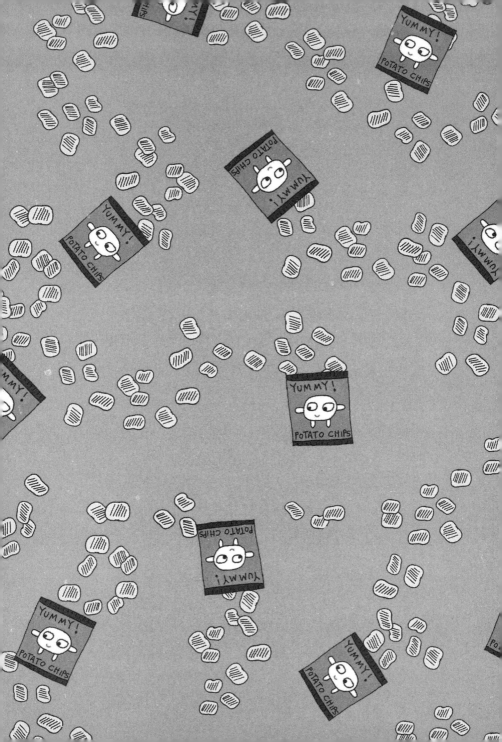

Just Grace and the Snack Attack

Written and illustrated
by
Charise Mericle Harper

Houghton Mifflin Books for Children

Houghton Mifflin Harcourt
Boston New York 2009

Houghton Mifflin Books for Children is an imprint of
Houghton Mifflin Harcourt Publishing Company.

www.hmhbooks.com

The text of this book is set in Dante.
The illustrations are pen and ink drawings digitally colored in Photoshop.

Library of Congress Cataloging-in-Publication Data is on file.
ISBN 978-0-547-15223-3

Manufactured in the United States of America
MP 10 9 8 7 6 5 4 3 2 1

This book is dedicated to the very lovely Kissy, who has enriched our lives with her presence, good humor, and style!

SOME UNEXPECTED GOOD THINGS

1 Finding money on the sidewalk.

2 Getting all the words right on your spelling test even though you forgot to study.

3 Meeting a famous person.

WHAT YOU DO WHEN AN UNEXPECTED GOOD THING HAPPENS TO YOU

Say a quiet-to-yourself thank-you.

QUIET THANK-YOUS VS. OUT-LOUD THANK-YOUS

Out-loud thank-yous are the kind you say when someone gives you a present or passes the ketchup across the table. These are important because it is always nice to be polite and thoughtful, but sometimes the biggest, most special thank-yous are the kind you say to yourself so no one else can hear you. These kind of thank-yous are probably the kind that would be nice to hear, but for some reason most people hardly ever say them.

Before school today I had three quiet thank-yous, but then an unexpected thing happened and now I have four. When something like this happens you can't help but think . . . *Today is going to be a great day!*

MY QUIET THANK-YOUS

1 Thank you, Mimi, for being the best friend in the whole world that a person could ever have.

2 Thank you, Miss Lois, for trying to be a more fun teacher like Mr. Frank, and not so bossy and not-smiling like you used to be.

3 *Merci* (which is French for "thank you"), Augustine Dupre, for having super-great ideas all the time and living in the nice apartment in my basement.

4 And finally, thank you, Owen 1, for picking on Sunni and saying that her lunch was disgusting and looked like worms.

WHY I AM THANKING OWEN 1

My thank-you to Owen 1 is a quiet thank-you, and one that I would never in two hundred thousand years say out loud so he could hear me.

At lunch today Owen 1 told Sunni that her lunch looked like worms, and that she was weird for not eating a sandwich like everyone else. Normally this is not a good thing, and it was even more of a not-good thing for Owen 1 because Mr. Harris, the principal of the school, was walking right behind Owen 1 when he said it. After Owen 1 got into lots of trouble, and after lunch was over, Mr. Harris sent a special note to Miss Lois. And now for the rest of the week, we are going to study foods of the world instead of the insides of frogs. Miss Lois said we are going to do this because it's important to appreciate people from other cultures and the interesting foods that they eat. No matter what anyone eats I am sure it cannot be as disgusting and gross as the insides of a frog. So thank you, Owen 1, because your not-good thing is now all of a sudden my great thing.

FROG VS. FOODS OF THE WORLD

WHY I AM NOT SAD FOR SUNNI

Sunni is super smart, and no matter what Owen 1 could say, it would probably never in a million years hurt her feelings. If Miss Lois said something mean to Sunni she would for sure cry, but Owen 1 does not have any make-Sunni-sad power. And probably Miss Lois would never say anything mean to Sunni anyway, because one, she is a teacher, and because two, Sunni is her number-one star student of the class. She pretty much never does anything wrong.

Sunni was not upset about Owen 1 calling her lunch disgusting. She just put one of the little round things she was eating in her mouth and stuck her tongue out at him. Mr. Harris didn't see that part.

Mimi said Sunni was eating a squid, but I didn't see any of those suction cup things or long skinny squid legs. It just looked like she was eating giant white Cheerios.

THE POOR OWENS

Every time Owen 1 does something dumb, which is a lot and more than you could really imagine, my empathy power starts feeling a little sad for the other two Owens in our class. They are the good Owens, and are probably mad that Owen 1 is messing up their Owen name. Sometimes when you start thinking a certain way about a person, it is hard not to think that same way about other people who have the exact same name. This can happen even if you know it's not fair — a little piece of your brain just wonders if those other boys with the Owen name are troublemakers too!

That's why I'm glad that the three other Graces in our class are nice, and I'm super glad that Grace F. turned out to *not* be the

Big Meanie that I first thought she was. This way I know no one is even thinking of having wondering thoughts about me.

THINGS THAT OWEN 1 DOES

1 Loud talking when he should be listening.

2 Not listening.

3 Kicking his desk when Miss Lois is reading, which makes it hard to concentrate on what she is saying because your ears keep hearing *bang, bang, bang* instead.

4 Trying to sneak-eat snacks when it is classtime and we are not allowed to be eating.

5 Saying mean things.

6 Always asking to go to the bathroom.

7 Chewing on his pencil like a beaver.

NORMAL PENCIL   **OWEN 1'S PENCIL**

MISSING PART OF PENCIL.

DOES HE ACTUALLY SWALLOW THIS PART?

THINGS THAT OWEN 2 AND OWEN 3 DO

1 Listening.

2 Being funny. (Well, just Owen 3 is funny. Owen 2 is kind of quiet.)

3 Not making trouble.

4 Liking superheroes.

WHAT HAPPENED BEFORE OWEN 1 MADE FUN OF SUNNI

Every Monday Miss Lois is full of ideas and rules about what we are going to be doing for the rest of the week. She says this helps our brains to be prepared for what is coming up and gives us a chance to be excited about the rest of the week. Since today was Monday she told us all about how we were going to be learning about the inside workings of frogs, and how we were going to be amazed about the things we were going to find out and discover. She made it sound like we were going on a treasure hunt, but for sure there was not going to be interesting treasure like crowns or jewels or gold on the inside of frogs.

Mostly it was the boys who were excited about the frogs. I don't like the outsides of frogs, so I was pretty sure I wasn't going to be filled with joy about what the inside parts looked like either. The only good thing about the whole project was that we were not going to be looking inside real frogs. Miss Lois said only older grades did that sort of thing. We were going to use plastic models. This was definitely something else to be thankful about.

Since I am not planning to be a doctor or a veterinarian, or a scientist, it's probably not so important for me to be understanding how frogs work anyway.

WHAT HAPPENED AFTER OWEN 1 MADE FUN OF SUNNI

Miss Lois said that she was not prepared to study foods of the world, and because of that she had no big ideas about what we should do next. Then she asked us, our whole class, if we had any suggestions. Miss Lois is a teacher who always seems like she knows exactly what she is doing, so Miss Lois with her head empty of ideas was something new. Of course our class

had tons of suggestions. Kids are always filled with ideas, but kids are not always filled with good ideas. This is probably why kids get into more trouble than grownups.

SOME OF THE IDEAS

Miss Lois said these were not good ideas:

1 Fly the whole class around the world so we can try all sorts of new foods.

2 Take the class out to dinner at a different restaurant every night so we can try all sorts of new foods.

3 Have a fancy chef come to our class and make us all sorts of new foods.

4 Buy up anything weird from the grocery store and bring it to class and then try to eat it.

Miss Lois said these were good ideas:

1 Tell the class about interesting foods that we have eaten at home or at restaurants.

2 Find out what kids from other countries eat for lunch at school.

3 Find out about interesting snacks from around the world.

4 Have a snack party where we can try some new foods.

It took up most of the afternoon to have the class find the ideas that Miss Lois liked. Owen 1 didn't say anything the whole time.

← NO SOUND COMING FROM HIM AT ALL.

This was a totally new record for him. He didn't even ask to go to the bathroom. He was acting like a person who was feeling guilty, a person who knew that probably every boy in the whole class was mad about the frog thing. I bet if he could have suddenly had any superpower in the whole world he would have picked the superpower to be invisible and disappear. I know this because this is exactly how I feel when I'm in trouble.

THE NEW IDEA IN MISS LOIS'S HEAD

Miss Lois said that we could keep a diary of interesting foods we ate, find out about snack foods from around the world, or find out what kids from other countries ate for lunch. Of course, she also had the big idea that we had to write everything we find out down, on at least two sheets of paper.

Miss Lois says she loves to save the earth, but I think she likes us to use up paper writing reports even more. For once, though, she said that we did not have to stand in front of the class and read our reports out loud. This was a good thing, because sometimes it gets pretty boring listening to everyone do their talks, especially certain people who are not very good at doing reports.

MISS LOIS'S BEST IDEA

Next Monday we get to have a snack party! Sandra Orr said she wanted to bring in some of her mom's famous Rice Krispie treats, but Miss Lois said we were not going to have that kind of snack party. Miss Lois said the snacks we were going to eat had to be unusual and different, and then we made a list of regular snacks so that no one else would be confused.

Miss Lois is smart about stuff like that —
certain people in our class get confused really
easily. Sometimes it seems like they don't
even understand English, which of course is
crazy, because that is the only language I hear
them speaking.

REGULAR SNACKS THAT CANNOT COME TO THE SNACK PARTY

Rice Krispie treats

Pretzels

Potato chips

Apple slices

Normal fruits

Regular cookies

Carrots

Raisins

Brownies

Cupcakes

The list could have gone on forever, because our class was excellent at thinking of all kinds of regular snacks, but Miss Lois finally said we had to stop.

Sandra Orr put her hand up again and asked if she could bring the Rice Krispie treats if her mom used food coloring to make them blue or green. That way they would be unusual and different but still taste delicious. Miss Lois seemed frustrated, because she said no in her tired voice. Sandra Orr was not upset, so I could just tell that her little brain was thinking about asking, "What if we color them yellow or red?" She is one of the people who have a hard time understanding simple instructions. Miss Lois must have been thinking the same thing as I was, because she said, "Regular snacks of any different color are not going to count as unusual snacks."

"What about unusual flavors of regular snacks?" Robert Walters did not put his hand up. "Like maybe tuna fish cupcakes?" Miss Lois gave Robert her you-need–to-put–your-hand-up look, but then she smiled and said, "Robert, if you are willing to eat a tuna fish cupcake, I will be more than happy to let you bring one to the snack party." Robert shook his head no, and then while everyone else was making "ewww" and "ugghhh" sounds, the bell rang to go home.

TUNA FISH CUPCAKE

WALKING HOME WITH MIMI

Right away Mimi said she was feeling just like me, happy that the frog project was canceled. We are both not big fans of frogs, or snakes, lizards, or any other reptiles. I didn't know Sammy was right behind us, because I was surprised when he said, "I can't believe Owen 1 ruined everything!" It's no surprise that Sammy would say that, though, because Sammy is a boy who likes unusual things, unusual things like frog guts.

Sammy wanted to do a lot of complaining about Owen 1, but now that school was over I didn't even want to think about Owen 1 anymore. Mimi and I had more interesting stuff to talk about. Things like . . .

1 What had happened on *Unlikely Heroes* (our most favorite TV show ever) last night.

2 If her cousin Gwen was totally loving Sally, her new puppy.

3 What Augustine Dupre taught me how to say in French.

4 What I was hoping I was going to have for dinner.

5 Why our friend Max wasn't at school.

6 What Mimi was hoping to have for dinner.

7 And tons of other really interesting stuff.

But Sammy didn't care about any of our excellent topics. All he wanted to do was interrupt us and complain, and complain, and complain about Owen 1.

Owen 1 does a lot of annoying things, so Sammy had a lot to complain about. He talked from the time we left school all the way until we arrived at Mimi's house, and still he wasn't finished. Sometimes when someone does this much complaining it's easy to get into a bad mood with them and start complaining too. This might have happened if we were frog lovers like Sammy, but we weren't, so this time we were pretty happy about Owen 1's troublemaking ways.

Even though I didn't want to, I felt a little sorry for Sammy. It's no fun to be grumpy all by yourself. It's like being under a tiny rain cloud when the whole rest of the

world is filled with sunshine. It's frustrating. Maybe Max would be angry with Owen 1 too, and then Sammy and Max could be happily grumpy together.

MIMI'S HOUSE

Mimi's mom loves making banana bread. She makes tons of it. Mimi says she does it because baking banana bread makes their house smell sweet and delicious — plus it's a good way to use up old bananas that no one wants to eat anymore, the kind that have black stuff on their skin and are super mushy inside. I hate them when they are like that.

At Mimi's house we are allowed to put butter and even jam on banana bread. I can't do this at my house. Mom doesn't believe in the "bread" part of banana bread. She says banana bread should really be called banana cake, and you don't need to put extra stuff on cake. It's 100 percent better to eat banana bread over at Mimi's house.

WHAT TASTES GOOD WITH BANANA BREAD

MIMI'S ROOM

After snacks we went up to Mimi's room. Mimi has the messiest room ever, but thankfully it doesn't smell messy. It smells clean. Mimi is not allowed to eat food in her bedroom and that is probably a good thing, because Mimi is the kind of girl who would leave food in strange and unexpected places.

There was a package on Mimi's bed. Right away we could tell it was from Gwen, Mimi's cousin, because the outside of the package had about twenty owls drawn all over it. Gwen's favorite animal is the owl. She pretty much decorates everything she owns with owls, so it's always easy to tell if something is from her.

Mimi is not a careful opener of presents

and packages, so it only took her about two seconds to rip it open. Inside was a sew-your-own-stuffed-animals kit, which was a 100 percent perfect present for Mimi.

The last time Gwen had stayed at Mimi's house she had fallen in love with Mimi's favorite stuffed animal, Willoughby. When it happened Mimi was super sad because she thought for sure that Gwen was going to keep Willoughby forever and never give him back. Lucky for her that didn't happen because Gwen got a surprise real puppy present, and that made her totally forget about her love for Willoughby. Mimi was lucky.

When someone gives you a present that you love that is perfect for you, it means that they have been paying attention to the kinds of things you like. This paying attention is part of the present too, because it means that the present giver really cares about you.

CUTE HANDLE ON THE BOX

MAKE YOUR OWN FRIENDS

SEW FUN

FUN

ALL SUPPLIES INCLUDED

Mimi was super excited about Gwen's present. She likes craft-type projects. She's not crazy about drawing, but she loves making things that you can hold on to, things that can stand up, and things that are not just pictures.

DRAWING BY ME

BUTTON EYES

TISSUE PAPER PETALS

PIPE CLEANERS

FLOWER BY MIMI

WHO CAN ABSOLUTELY NOT SEW

ME!

WHO CAN ABSOLUTELY NOT SEW, EVEN IF SHE TRIES SUPER HARD

ME!

WHO THINKS I COULD MAYBE SEW IF I TRIED HARDER

Mimi, but she is wrong!

Mimi was giving me her look-at-this-fun-project-we-can-do-together look. We practice our looks a lot, so mostly I am pretty good at figuring out what Mimi is going to say before she even says it. "Do you want to make one with me?" asked Mimi. I shook my head in a big no. I have ten fingers and no thumbs when it comes to sewing. You can't sew if you only have fingers! Thumbs are important. Sometimes Mimi pretends to forget that I'm completely hopeless at using anything that is in the string family. This includes knitting, sewing, crocheting, embroidery, and even tying ribbons on presents.

HANDS
WITH NO THUMBS

← YOU CAN'T GRAB ANYTHING.

WHY THIS IS REALLY TOO BAD

Mostly I don't feel bad about having two extra fingers and no thumbs, but when I saw how cute the make-your-own stuffed animals were I felt a little sad for me and my not being able to sew. They were really cute.

Mimi was holding up the box and making it dance in front of me, hoping that I was going to say, "Okay, I'll make one too." But I couldn't  say that. "Mimi, you know I'll just wreck it if I try to sew it." Mimi looked disappointed, but she knew what I was saying was 100 percent true. I can draw comics like crazy, but I cannot even sew on a button.

WHAT MIMI WANTED TO DO NEXT

Mimi could not wait to start sewing. She said we could talk about other stuff, but really what she mostly wanted to do was to start stuffing! I watched her for a little while but then decided to go home and see what we were having for dinner. It's not that much fun watching someone else working on something. Kind of like watching me draw. How fun would that be?

WHAT WE WERE HAVING FOR DINNER

Mom made her rice and sausage casserole for dinner. Not bad, but not something super great and exciting.

SAUSAGES
ON TOP OF RICE

(IT'S ACTUALLY MORE YUMMY THAN IT LOOKS)

At dinner I told Mom and Dad about Miss Lois's new project at school and how it had all happened. Mom said that she hoped I wasn't making fun of Sunni too. Of course I told her she would never have to worry about that. I am not the kind of girl that does things like that. Mom said that sometimes children act out because they need attention. Owen 1 must be 100 percent starving for attention, because he acts out all the time. This is one of those things you can't tell about a person just by looking at them, but if you spent some time with Owen 1 you would for sure be able to guess it.

Dad said he thought our school project sounded like fun. He said, "You kids are so lucky. I didn't even try Japanese food until I was twenty-two years old." Then Mom said she was about that old when she tried Indian food for the first time. I guess eating wasn't that exciting when they were kids.

After dinner we made a list of all the kinds of foods I have tried so far in my life. Mom said I had a very international palate. That means my mouth has tasted foods from all over the world, even though my body has mostly stayed home.

MY MOUTH IS A WORLD TRAVELER

FOODS I HAVE TRIED AND MOSTLY LIKED

Thai food. I like pad thai, which is a noodle thing with peanuts on it, but I don't like it when it is spicy. I also like pad se ew, which is another noodley thing, but the noodles are big and chewy, which makes it more fun to eat.

Chinese food. I pretty much like all the Chinese food I have tried. I especially like moo shoo because you get to fill up your own little pancake and then put the yummy plum sauce on top.

Korean food. I have only tried bulgogi, but I liked it a lot. It's a beef thing that has been marinated in a special yummy sauce.

Italian food. I love every kind of pasta ever invented! Even pasta with clam sauce, which is sort of an unusual thing for a kid to like. Noodles, the not-cooked kind, are also really good for making craft projects. This is pretty much the only food parents let you play with when you are little.

SOME KINDS OF NOODLES

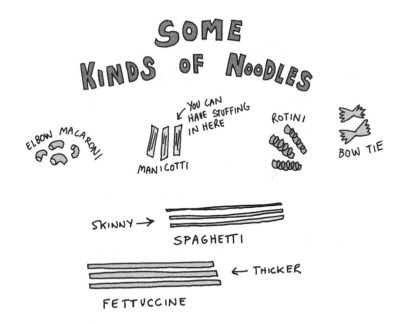

French food. Augustine Dupre once made us some French snails. I tried really hard, but I couldn't even make myself taste them. Mom said they were delicious, but I just ate the French bread that they came with. I also really like croissants with strawberry jam. So mostly I only like French bread products.

Japanese food. My favorite Japanese food is sushi. It's good to eat, plus it's pretty to look at. Sushi rolls kind of look like mini round sandwich wraps, but instead of tortillas holding everything in, they use seaweed and rice. I love California rolls, and tempura rolls, and even salmon and avocado rolls. I also really like edamame, which is a green pea-bean-like thing.

Indian food. I like the nan bread and the yummy tomato sauce with the square cheese in it. It's called paneer butter masala, which is a long name for just one thing.

Greek food. We once had Greek chicken and potatoes at a Greek restaurant in the city. Mom said she was going to try to make us the same thing at home, but so far she hasn't done it.

MOM'S BIG IDEA

Mom said we should try some new kind of food for dinner on Friday night. Something different and unusual that we haven't had before. Sometimes Mom can be a little too filled with adventure when it comes to trying new foods. The last time she tried to make us something new and unusual it turned into a disaster. She tried to make country garden veggie balls, and they turned out awful. Mom said they were supposed to be soft and moist, but they ended up being hard, grainy, and dry. Dad said it was like trying to eat salty, stale mini cake donuts. After a couple of tiny bites even Mom said, "I can't eat this!" Dad was happy to go out and get us a pizza instead.

HARD VEGGIE BALLS OR DELICIOUS PIZZA

Dad must have been remembering that dinner too, because he said we should go out to eat: that way we could experience the new food in an interesting new environment and Mom wouldn't have to cook. Since Dad was in such a good mood, I asked if Mimi could come too. "Why not," said Dad, "as long as she is willing to try something new." "She totally is! Mimi loves new foods." I said this even though I didn't really know if it was true or not, or what we were going to be eating. Sometimes best friends can still be learning new stuff about each other, even if it seems like they have been together forever.

WHAT I DID AFTER DINNER

Mom does not like me spending too much time visiting with Augustine Dupre. Mom thinks that mostly I bother Augustine Dupre with my chitchatting and that Augustine Dupre is probably too nice to ask me to leave her alone. Mom is wrong. I know for certain that Augustine Dupre likes to talk with me. She lives all alone in our basement — who else is she going to talk to? Plus, we are friends.

Because of Mom's crazy thinking, I have to sneak down the stairs to visit her. I always give Augustine Dupre's door a secret knock so she will know it is me. As soon as I did my knock Augustine Dupre opened the door and let me in. She was eating dinner, and I was happy that it was not snails. It's not easy to watch someone eat something you think is disgusting.

"I have a little present for you," she said. Then she rummaged around in her suitcase. Augustine Dupre is a flight attendant, so she is always being glamorous and flying off to France. While she was looking for the present I went and sat on her sofa next to Crinkles.

Crinkles is my next-door neighbor Mrs. Luther's cat, but he is in love with Augustine Dupre. He is not supposed to be in her apartment because Dad has a crazy no-pets rule, but I would never in a million years say anything to get them into trouble. It's nice for Augustine Dupre to have a furry, purry body to be cozy with.

MY PRESENT

Augustine Dupre was right about the present being little. At first I was disappointed, because it seemed like the whole present was just a piece of paper. But after we looked at it together and she explained it, I was a lot more excited. Augustine Dupre said that the little paper was called a zine, and that zines were popular with people who liked to draw comics and tell stories. People just like me. It was a way for artists to make photocopies of their comics and turn them into cute little books.

FRENCH.
IT MEANS
"THE CAT"

FOLDED-
UP LITTLE
BOOK THAT
YOU CAN MAKE
FROM A
PIECE OF
REGULAR PAPER

Since the zine was in French, Augustine Dupre had to explain the story to me. It seemed a little like a Tom and Jerry story, because the cat was getting beat up by the mouse a lot. I'm not a big fan of Tom and Jerry, so mostly I liked the idea of the zine more than I liked the story. Augustine Dupre helped me unfold it and then put it back together again so I could see how to make one myself. It was a great present, and now I was feeling a little guilty that I didn't show more excitement when she first gave it to me. I don't know if Augustine Dupre noticed that or not, but I was hoping that she hadn't.

HOW TO MAKE A ZINE

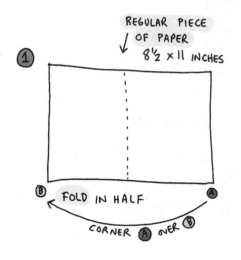

REGULAR PIECE OF PAPER
8½ × 11 INCHES

① FOLD IN HALF
CORNER Ⓐ OVER Ⓑ

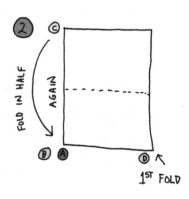

② FOLD IN HALF AGAIN
1ST FOLD

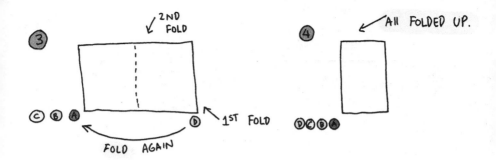

③ 2ND
   FOLD
   1ST FOLD
   FOLD AGAIN

④ All FOLDED UP.

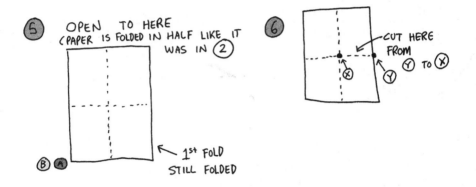

⑤ OPEN TO HERE
    (PAPER IS FOLDED IN HALF LIKE IT WAS IN ②)
    1st FOLD STILL FOLDED

⑥ CUT HERE FROM
    Ⓨ TO Ⓧ

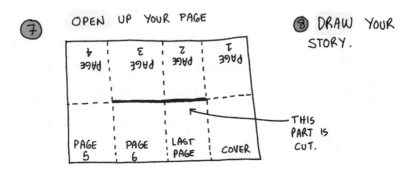

⑦ OPEN UP YOUR PAGE

    PAGE 4   PAGE 3   PAGE 2   PAGE 1

    PAGE 5   PAGE 6   LAST PAGE   COVER

    THIS PART IS CUT.

⑧ DRAW YOUR STORY.

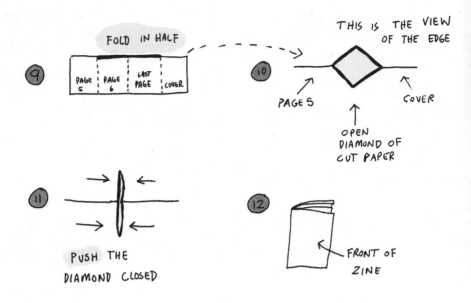

9 FOLD IN HALF

| PAGE 5 | PAGE 6 | LAST PAGE | COVER |

10 THIS IS THE VIEW OF THE EDGE

PAGES

OPEN DIAMOND OF CUT PAPER

COVER

11 PUSH THE DIAMOND CLOSED

12 FRONT OF ZINE

"This is a great present. I love it. Thank you!" I was 100 percent happy, and I hoped that she knew that my joy was for real and not made up. Sometimes you have to pretend to be happy about a present even if you don't really like it. That's because it's important to help the present giver feel good about thinking about you and giving you something, but this was not one of those times. Just before

I left, Augustine Dupre gave me another present. It was a bag of French potato chips.

FRENCH CHIPS

(THESE ARE MUCH YUMMIER THAN YOU WOULD MAYBE THINK.)

WHAT YOU SHOULD NOT DO AT NIGHT RIGHT BEFORE GOING TO BED

Try one potato chip from a bag with a picture of a roasted chicken on the front of it.

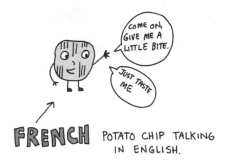

FRENCH POTATO CHIP TALKING IN ENGLISH.

WHY YOU SHOULD NOT DO THIS

Because these kind of potato chips are delicious, and soon you will have to eat more and more until the whole bag is completely empty, and then you will be very thirsty. All night you will be very, very thirsty.

MUST HAVE WATER!

WHAT I LOOKED FOR AT NIGHT

When I was getting one of my drinks of water I looked to see if Mimi was maybe up too. My window is right across from hers, so we can wave to each other, and even do secret codes if we are both looking at the same time. I was 100 percent surprised to see a little bit of a light on in her room. It wasn't her normal big light, but something small like maybe a flashlight or a book light. I flashed my light a couple of times to try to get her attention, but she was not looking, or maybe she had fallen asleep. I was going to have to ask her about that.

WHAT WOULD BE REALLY GREAT

Forever Mimi and I have been wanting to get a pulley thing that goes from her window all the way to my window. It would be perfect for us. We could send stuff back and forth, and maybe even have a little bell so that we would know when the other person was looking for us to be ready at the window. I once saw something exactly like that on a TV show. It had a little basket attached to it and the two people were sending notes, food, and even a cat back and forth. Of course, Mimi and I could never send a cat because she is allergic to cats, and Crinkles would for sure hate being in a basket way above the ground. Plus, he's not even my cat. Ever since I first told Mimi about the pulley, we have been wishing we could have one for ourselves.

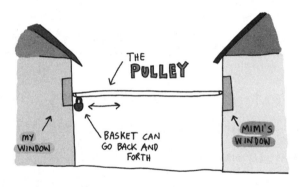

THE PULLEY

MY WINDOW

BASKET CAN GO BACK AND FORTH

MIMI'S WINDOW

The sad thing that is for sure is that Mimi's dad would never let us attach something like a pulley to their house. He is not that kind of dad. He is very serious about having his house and his grass be perfectly perfect. It would probably drive him crazy to see a line hanging up there in the air over his lawn. It's too bad, though, because something like that would be 100 percent amazing, fun, and useful.

THE TWO THINGS I WOKE UP THINKING

1 *I really need another drink of water.*

2 *I could do my project about potato chips.*

WHAT HAPPENED BEFORE SCHOOL

Dad was sitting at breakfast reading the newspaper. This was a good thing, because Sammy is our newspaper boy and mostly he used to be really bad about getting the newspaper to our house on time. This would make Dad grumpy in the morning, and it's no fun to eat breakfast with a grumpy dad.

I wanted to talk about potato chips, but

Dad just wanted to read the paper. I guess that was Sammy's fault for getting it to our house on time. Mom was not like Dad. Mom was very happy to talk about potato chips. She said her favorite flavor was sour cream and onion, and that when she was young she used to love salt and vinegar chips. She said they tasted especially good when you smooshed them inside a tuna sandwich. I'm not a big lover of tuna, so that sounded pretty gross to me.

I asked her if she had ever heard of roast-chicken-flavored potato chips. I couldn't tell her that I had eaten a whole bag of those exact chips the night before, because I couldn't tell her that I had been to visit Augustine Dupre when I was not supposed to. Suddenly there was a lot I couldn't say. Mom said that roast chicken sounded strange, but she had once tried pickle-flavored chips and they were pretty good. Yuck! I hate pickles. Mom and I obviously do not have potato chip flavors in common.

WHAT DAD SAID RIGHT WHEN I WAS LEAVING

"I once tried ketchup-flavored chips and they were disgusting."

WHAT MIMI HAD TO SHOW ME

I was going to tell Mimi all about my potato chip adventure and project idea, but she was too excited about her new stuffed animals to be a good listener. Now I knew why her light was on so late. She had totally finished all of the three stuffed animals that were in the kit. She said her fingers were sore from pushing the needle but that it was worth all the trouble. Her stuffed animals were cute, but I'm glad my fingers weren't the ones all bandaged up.

MIMI'S CREATIONS

MY IDEA

Mostly it's good to try to come up with an idea for a project right when you first find out about it. This is because as time goes by, all the good ideas get taken up by other people and then you're left with all the boring stuff like researching yogurt or carrot sticks. I was telling this to Mimi so she would start to think about our assignment and then we could maybe talk some more about my idea, but she was not interested. She said, "I can't think about that right now." Her brain was too filled up with thinking about making more stuffed animals. It was like she was poisoned with craftiness.

WHAT MISS LOIS SAID

Miss Lois said, "I have been doing my homework about interesting foods of the world — have you?" Then she looked around the class to see if people were smiling or if they were trying to make themselves invisible and disappear.

OWEN 3 TRYING TO DISAPPEAR

I got the feeling that most people were wishing that Miss Lois would not be able to see them. This is a wish you have when you have not done your homework or you do not know the answer to a question. Sunni put her hand up, but that was no surprise because she always has her hand up and she always knows the answers to everything. Miss Lois looked around the room to see if anyone else wanted to talk too. Miss Lois usually does this before she lets Sunni talk. This is a good thing, because if she didn't look for other people, it would just be her and Sunni talking by themselves all day long.

I was thinking about telling Miss Lois about my potato chip idea but I wanted to hear what Sunni was going to say first. If she was going to pick potato chips as her project, then I was for sure going to pick something else. Only a crazy person would pick the same project idea as Sunni. Even if you tried really hard this is what would happen.

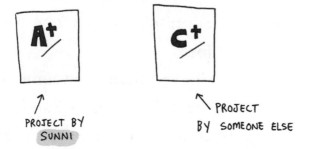

PROJECT BY
SUNNI

PROJECT
BY SOMEONE ELSE

WHAT I WAS HAPPY ABOUT

Sunni said she was going to keep a journal of foods that her family ate, because they pretty much ate unusual things all the time. She was going to photograph her supper plate every night and then make a diagram of what all the different foods were. Miss Lois said that was a great idea, and that she was sure that everyone in the class was going to find the different foods very interesting. Mostly I was happy because Sunni did not say one word about potato chips.

Two seconds later Valerie Newcome put her hand up and said, "How come Sunni just has to take pictures of her dinner? That's like no work at all. It's not my fault that my family doesn't eat weird stuff." Suddenly lots of the other kids in our class were pretty much paying attention. I could tell that some of them were thinking the exact same thing as Valerie, because they were nodding their heads up and down like you do when you agree about something. Even though Valerie was complaining, Miss Lois must have been a little bit impressed with her, because usually Valerie doesn't pay enough attention to even ask a smart question.

Miss Lois said that she was sure that Sunni was going to hand in more than photos of her dinner plates, and then she asked Valerie what she was planning to do as a project. Valerie didn't say anything, so it was obvious that she had not been doing any planning at all. Sometimes this is true of complainers. Miss Lois looked around the class and then she said she wanted to show us some interesting and unusual fruits of the world.

FRUITS

It's kind of weird to think that there are all sorts of fruits that I have never even heard of or tried. These are the fruits Miss Lois showed us.

THE FRUITS

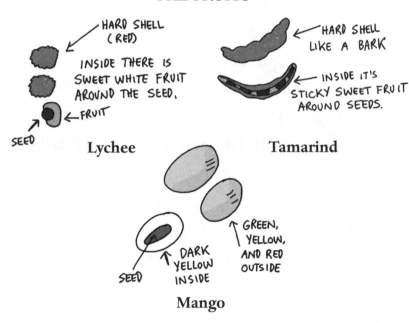

HARD SHELL (RED)

INSIDE THERE IS SWEET WHITE FRUIT AROUND THE SEED.

FRUIT

SEED

Lychee

HARD SHELL LIKE A BARK

INSIDE IT'S STICKY SWEET FRUIT AROUND SEEDS.

Tamarind

GREEN, YELLOW, AND RED OUTSIDE

DARK YELLOW INSIDE

SEED

Mango

(I knew this one.)

WHAT I COULD NOT BELIEVE

I could not believe that some of the kids in our class had never tried or even seen a mango. Mangoes are not that unusual — plus, they are 100 percent delicious. I put my hand up as soon as Miss Lois asked if anyone had ever tried one. Owen 1 looked like he was about to say something, but then he put his hand over his mouth real quick before any sound could come out. It almost looked like he was choking, but I think he was just trying to keep his words inside.

WHICH IS HARDER

Looking at Owen 1 made me wonder if he has a harder time with his life than Owen 2 or Owen 3 does. Owen 1 is always doing or saying dumb stuff that gets him into trouble. It's like his brain is a volcano of bad ideas. He does not at all make good choices.

The other two Owens don't have this problem — they do good things without even looking like they have to think about it. They do not have to swallow their words every ten seconds to keep from getting into trouble. This made me feel a tiny bit of my empathy feelings for Owen 1. It was not a lot, not even enough that anyone could ever know about it except me.

WHAT HAPPENED NEXT

Miss Lois let everyone touch and look at the fruits she had brought. She said we were going to be allowed to taste them at our snack party. I didn't say anything about it, but I was hoping that the fruits we were going to be eating were going to be new ones. I was 100 percent sure I didn't want to be eating these fruits that everyone was touching. They were definitely germ filled. Yuck.

EATING LUNCH

Mimi and I sat with Grace F. and Jordan at lunchtime. Normally Jordan has to sit with her class, but she snuck over to our table and no one seemed to notice. Jordan is my gym partner. Our class always has gym with Mrs.

Koppel's class, which is Jordan's class. I was lucky to get Jordan as a gym partner, because she is really good at running, and jumping, and catching stuff, and she doesn't seem to mind that I am not that good at any of those things. She is the fastest runner in the class, so it's kind of funny that she is also the slowest eater in the world.

Practically our whole table had finished eating and she was still working on her sandwich. That was probably why Grace F. noticed what she was eating. "What kind of sandwich is that?" she asked. "Hot dog, cream cheese, and pickles," said Jordan. "You could win a weird-sandwich award," said Grace F. "How can you eat a cold hot dog with that

other stuff on it?" "Lots of people eat weird stuff on their hot dogs," said Jordan, and then she smiled.

Jordan kind of likes to be different from everybody else. She says it makes her stand out and that that kind of thing is important when you are shorter than most everyone in the whole class. What she said about weird stuff on hot dogs was true too, because in Chicago my dad ate a hot dog with all sorts of crazy stuff on it. I was thinking about all this when Mimi suddenly said, "Hey, I can do my report about hot dogs of the world!" And that is exactly how Mimi came up with her food project idea.

MY AFTERNOON SURPRISE

Owen 1 did not get into any trouble all afternoon. When Miss Lois was reading us some instructions, he did not annoy us with kicking the desk or ask to go to the bathroom every five minutes. This was a new record for him. It was almost like Owen 1 was a whole new Owen. It was a mystery why he was being so good. Maybe he had finally used up all his annoying energy.

Miss Lois asked everyone who had already thought of a project idea to write it down on a piece of paper and hand it in. Then she copied the ideas onto the big board at the front of the class. So far the ideas were . . .

Foods on a stick.

Insects that people eat. (This one sounded disgusting.)

Hot dogs of the world.

Unusual ice creams.

A food diary.

A food diary. (Two people had a food diary, but Miss Lois said that was okay because she was pretty sure they would turn out to be different.)

Unusual potato chips of the world. (This one was mine.)

There was no wondering about who had written the insects idea. It sounded like 100 percent Sammy Stringer to me.

WHAT WE STUDIED AFTER THAT

After that Miss Lois had us study regular stuff like we normally did. I was disappointed because I was hoping this was not going to happen. I wanted to forget about fractions, and spelling, and history and all our regular work for the whole rest of the week. Miss Lois obviously wasn't 100 percent in love with the foods of the world idea like I was.

THE GOOD THING THAT HAPPENED IN THE AFTERNOON

We got a postcard from Mr. Frank. This was surprising for all of us, because we didn't even know that he was on vacation. Mr. Frank used to be our student teacher, and pretty much our favorite teacher ever. He was young, so he was more like us, always full of energy and ideas. His postcard was from a place called the Dominican Republic. Miss Lois showed us where it was on the map, and I was surprised to find out it was an island. She said Mr. Frank was on a special trip where he was teaching English to children who mostly spoke Spanish. Miss Lois said it was all very exciting.

When Miss Lois read Mr. Frank's postcard to the class I could tell that everyone was really excited to hear it, because we were all super quiet and paying extra-good attention. This kind of thing does not happen very often. Mr. Frank said he missed everyone and was hoping to come back for a visit when he finished his trip. That way he could tell us all about the Dominican Republic. He said he slept under a special tent at night so that the bugs couldn't bite him, and that he was hoping to see some humpback whales in the ocean. The whale part sounded cool, but I was pretty sure I wouldn't like it there, mostly because of the biting bugs part.

GOOD

NOT GOOD

Miss Lois said she was going to go home and research the foods of the Dominican Republic — that way we could all talk about the kinds of things Mr. Frank was eating. Owen 1 put his hand up and said that Mr. Frank was probably eating fried spiders, because he had seen a show on TV that showed a place with palm trees, and the people living there really liked to eat fried tarantulas. Mr. Frank's postcard had a palm tree on the front, but Miss Lois said she was pretty sure that most people who lived near palm trees didn't eat tarantulas.

GIANT SPIDER
(TARANTULA)

I thought about telling her about how people sometimes ate spiders by accident, when they were sleeping with their mouths

BIG SPIDER

open, but that kind of thing probably didn't happen with tarantulas. They were too big.

WALKING HOME WITH MIMI

Mimi said she was going to ask my dad to help her with her hot dog project since he is a big lover of hot dogs. Her dad doesn't like hot dogs, so he is not a hot dog expert. I told her I wasn't sure how helpful Dad was going to be, because just this morning he was pretty much no help at all when I wanted to talk about potato chips.

WHAT MIMI WANTED AFTER SCHOOL

After school Mimi and I went to my house. Normally we would have had a snack in the kitchen before going up to my room, but for some reason Mimi wanted to skip the snack.

As soon as we sat on my bed, she asked me if I had any old clothes I wanted to get rid of. This was a strange question for Mimi to ask. This was not Mimi being normal. I did not answer Mimi's question right away because I was trying to think about why she was even asking me something like this. Lucky for me, Mimi couldn't see inside my brain. She was probably thinking I was making a list of all my clothes and trying to decide if I wanted them anymore or not. But she was wrong. I was not doing this.

WHAT MY BRAIN WAS THINKING

1 Mimi wants to collect things to have another yard sale. We had done that once, but Mimi couldn't say goodbye to any of her stuff, so she didn't sell anything.

2 Mimi wants to trade clothes with me. This would not be a super-great idea because we are not exactly the same size.

3 Mimi is crazy. I wasn't really thinking this except for a super-fast second. It wasn't a real thought, just something that went past my brain really fast, like a racecar or a rocket.

WHAT HAPPENED NEXT

All this must have been taking a long time because Mimi finally interrupted my thinking and said, "I'm just looking for material so I can make some more stuffed animals." What she said was a surprise, and not one of the things I had thought of. Sometimes even your best friend can 100 percent surprise you.

WHAT WAS TOO BAD FOR MIMI

I don't have any clothes I can't wear because every couple of months Mom goes through my closet and picks out the clothes that don't fit me anymore. She sends all my old things to a friend of hers who has two little twin girls. They don't live near us, but if they ever come to visit it will be strange, because they will be wearing my clothes.

WHAT HAPPENED AFTER THAT

Mimi said she had changed her mind and now she definitely wanted to go downstairs and have a snack after all. I could tell she was disappointed about the material thing but was hoping that maybe a couple of cookies would make her feel better.

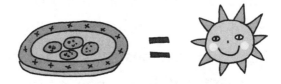

WHAT WAS A BIG SURPRISE FOR ME

Mimi stayed until Dad got home from work. He must have been in a great mood, because as soon as Mimi said she was doing her food project about hot dogs he offered to help her. Even though she is my best friend, this made me a little grumpy. A dad is supposed to help his daughter first, not his daughter's best friend. Now suddenly he was using all his helping energy on Mimi instead of me.

I'm a good actor, though, because I smiled like I was happy that Dad was helping Mimi, and they couldn't see the truth, and the truth was that I was mostly feeling jealous.

This is not a comfortable feeling to have. It's like wearing a super-scratchy sweater but pretending it's as soft as bunny fur so no one will notice.

WHY JEALOUS FEELINGS ARE NOT GOOD

They make you think not-nice feelings about people you love, like maybe even your best friend.

WHY JEALOUS FEELINGS ARE DANGEROUS

They might make you do not-nice things to try to make yourself feel better.

WHAT YOU SHOULD DO ABOUT JEALOUS FEELINGS

I have had jealous feelings before, so I know what to look out for. When you feel this way you have to be careful about what you say, because sometimes the words that want to come out of your mouth are not helpful and nice. Sometimes they are mean and harmful.

I had to be like Owen 1 and swallow my words. It's not easy to pretend smile when your inside feelings are hurt. I went to sit in the bathroom. I didn't have to smile in there.

WHAT DAD TOLD MIMI

I stayed in the bathroom a really long time, so long that I was sure that Dad and Mimi would be all done when I came out. I guess there is a lot to learn about hot dogs, because Mimi and Dad were still talking when I got back. Mimi was busy writing everything down on paper. She was for sure not going to have to do boring research about her project like I was. Dad was giving her all the answers to every hot dog question she could ever have — plus, they were even looking on the computer together. Dad said that he couldn't believe that people in Colombia eat hot dogs with crushed potato chips, cheese, ham, bacon, ketchup, mustard, mayonnaise, pineapple, and onion on them. I didn't say anything, but that sounded like a super-big stomachache to me!

Finally, when they were finished, Dad told Mimi he was looking forward to our adventure dinner on Friday. At first Mimi was confused, because I hadn't even invited her yet, but then after he explained it, she said of course she'd love to come. This was too bad, because I was kind of thinking of not inviting her anymore and now it was definitely too late for that.

FRIDAY SOUNDS LIKE SO MUCH FUN.

WHY SOMETIMES YOU HAVE TO LIE

Mom asked me if Mimi wanted to stay for dinner. This was a bit of a surprise since she usually doesn't let me have dinner guests on school nights. But before she could say anything else, I told her that Mimi had to go home to her own house for dinner. This was not true, but if Mimi stayed I was worried that I would maybe say something bad that would hurt her feelings. Not that it would 100 percent happen, but I had a feeling that on this kind of day, it could happen by accident.

After Mimi left I went upstairs to draw a comic. Drawing always makes me feel better, and I needed to feel better real fast. I made my first ever zine, just like the one Augustine Dupre gave me as a model. Somehow, having the comic be in a little book makes it feel so much more special than just having it on a piece of paper. I looked at it about a million times. This is probably what real authors do when they get their books for the first time. When you work really hard on something, it's nice to be able to hold all that hard work in your hands.

FRONT COVER **BACK COVER/LAST PAGE**

NOT SO SUPER

WHAT HAPPENED AT DINNER

We had sushi takeout for dinner. This made me feel guilty about sending Mimi home. Mimi's parents don't like sushi, so the only time she gets to eat it is if she's at our house. Now I wasn't feeling so much jealous anymore. I was just feeling more like a bad friend.

WHAT WAS DISAPPOINTING

1 That I was feeling so guilty about Mimi that it made me not hungry to enjoy my sushi dinner.

2 That Dad still did not want to talk about potato chips. He said he didn't know anything about them and that I should look them up on the computer.

3 That the restaurant forgot to put in the ginger candies they usually give you for dessert. They are my favorite!

4 That I still felt as yucky after dinner as I did before dinner.

THE THING I'M WONDERING ABOUT

I don't know why it happens this way, but it seems like it's always nighttime right when I really need to visit Augustine Dupre. Somehow all my problems seem bigger in the dark, when there is not so much other stuff going on to take my mind away from them. Augustine Dupre is excellent at solving problems, which is why I needed her right away.

I was lucky that one of Mom's favorite

shows was on — that way I was able to sneak downstairs without her seeing me. I had to knock a couple of times before Augustine Dupre opened the door. I thought she was maybe on the phone or something, but when she let me in I saw that she was just talking to Crinkles. He spends more time living with Augustine Dupre than he does with Mrs. Luther, and she is his owner.

WHAT I TOLD AUGUSTINE DUPRE

The first thing I had to tell Augustine Dupre was how absolutely amazing I thought the French chicken-flavored potato chips were. She said they were one of her favorites too, and that France had all kinds of interesting potato chip flavors. She said she also really liked olive-flavored potato chips, but that was one I was not going to like for sure. I'm not a big fan of olives.

The second thing I told Augustine Dupre was all about how Dad was helping Mimi and not helping me, and how that was making me feel mad at Mimi, even though it was completely not at all her fault.

She shook her head and said, "Friendships can be hard." This was not what I was wanting her to say, and not why I had snuck downstairs at seven o'clock at night to see her.

WHAT I WANTED
AUGUSTINE DUPRE TO SAY

1 "You are so right about feeling jealous. How dare your father tell Mimi all about hot dogs!"

2 "Your father should research potato chips for you. It's only fair, since he did all Mimi's homework for her."

3 "If Mimi was a true friend she would be able to tell you are feeling weird and jealous just by looking at you."

WHAT'S WRONG, GRACE? EVEN THOUGH YOU LOOK HAPPY I CAN TELL YOU ARE SAD.

WHAT WAS TOO BAD FOR ME

Augustine Dupre did not say any of these things.

WHAT AUGUSTINE DUPRE DID SAY

She said, "It takes a lifetime to learn all there is to know about another person. You need to be patient." Then she said that even my mom and dad, who have been together forever, were probably still learning new stuff about each other. I don't know if she was right about Mom and Dad, but she was right about Mimi and me. For sure Mimi was at her house sewing a fantastic stuffed animal and not knowing one bit at all that I was unhappy.

Usually a trip down to see Augustine Dupre makes me feel better, but I wasn't feeling any of her feel-better magic this time.

WHAT I HAVE TO DO AFTER VISITING AUGUSTINE DUPRE

Sneak back upstairs.

Once, before I knew better, I raced upstairs after sneaking down to visit Augustine Dupre. This was not good, because Mom was walking right at the top of the stairs when I opened the door. Of course she knew right away where I had been, and I got into big trouble for going downstairs without asking. I thought about trying to say that I had been down in the spidery part of the basement instead of the Augustine Dupre apartment part of the basement, but Mom would have never in a million years believed that. She knows me too well.

WHAT I KNOW ABOUT POTATO CHIPS NOW

1 Salty.

2 Delicious.

3 Lots of flavors.

WHAT I KNOW ABOUT POTATO CHIPS AFTER TWENTY MINUTES ON THE COMPUTER

1 Mostly salty.

There is a company that once tried to

sell fruit-flavored potato chips, but no one wanted to buy them so they stopped making them. Fruit-flavored chips don't sound as gross or as weird as some of the other flavors I found.

2 Maybe not all delicious.

There are some really strange flavors that don't sound very yummy.

3 Lots and lots of flavors.

I couldn't believe how many different potato chip flavors there are in the world. The research part was really easy. There is a lot of information about potato chips on the Internet. People just love potato chips.

4 March 14 is national potato chip day.

SOME COUNTRIES AND SOME POTATO CHIP FLAVORS

SOUTH AFRICA

Sausage, beef jerky, Worcestershire sauce.

CANADA

Dill pickle, ketchup, bacon, curry.

ENGLAND

In England, even though they speak English, they don't call potato chips potato chips. They call them crisps instead. And to make everything even more confusing, when they do say chips, they actually mean french fries.

They have lots of different flavors of crisps. They have roast chicken, probably like the French kind I already tried, which means they are delicious! Some of the other flavors are things like lamb and mint, ham and mustard, pickled onion, and mango chili, and there are lots more. Lots of flavors sounded like food you would eat for dinner. I wonder if people did that? Just eat chips (crisps) instead of dinner.

I'll START WITH THE HAM AND MUSTARD...

JAPAN
Seaweed and salt, wasabi (which is that spicy green paste they give you when you order sushi), soy sauce and butter, mayonnaise, cheese curry.

NEW ZEALAND
(THE COUNTRY NEXT TO AUSTRALIA)
Honey and soy chicken, smoked salmon and capers, chili and sour cream.

WHAT HAPPENS WHEN YOU DO POTATO CHIP RESEARCH

You get hungry.

Now I was wishing that I had saved some of those yummy French potato chips from last night. That kind of thing is really hard to do, though, because once you start eating chips, you pretty much want to keep going until the bag is empty. Maybe if the bag were bigger I would have saved some . . . or maybe I just would have eaten a bigger bag's worth. This is the kind of thing you just can't guess about until it is happening.

I CAN'T DO IT. I CAN'T STOP EATING THESE CHIPS.

WHAT I SAW OUT MY WINDOW

Mimi waving at me. I waved back, and suddenly I was feeling a lot better. She was holding and pointing at something but I couldn't tell what it was.

WHAT ALWAYS MAKES ME FEEL GOOD IN THE MORNING

I asked Mom for French toast, because I always like to have French toast for breakfast if I feel my empathy power working. I was still a little upset about yesterday and everything that had happened, but I was going to try to forget about it. I was going to forget about Dad not wanting to help me. I was going to forget about Mimi not noticing my feelings. I was going to forget about everything that was annoying me. I was going to start like brand new.

WHAT WAS A SURPRISE AT BREAKFAST

Mom said that Dad wanted to change our plans about Friday night and that we were going to eat at home instead of going out. She said he was all excited about a big new fun idea he had. This did not make me happy. It was not fair that Dad's idea was taking over our adventure dinner. Plus, I couldn't even ask him about it because he had gone to work early. My good day was not starting out so perfectly good.

WHAT I WONDER

I wonder if superheroes ever get dressed in their special superhero outfits and then when they finally step outside to start their day, they just wish they had stayed inside with their pajamas on instead. This is how I felt, only I wasn't wearing a special outfit — I was just full of French toast.

INSIDE THE HOUSE

OUTSIDE THE HOUSE

WHAT HAPPENED OUTSIDE

Usually Mimi and I walk to school together, but when I went to Mimi's house to get her, her mom said that she had already left. I couldn't believe it. We always wait for each other! Now I was really grumpy! Then, to make things even worse, Sammy showed up and wanted to walk with me. He said Max was still sick with a cold and wasn't going to be at school again. Poor Max. I didn't even know he was sick.

WHAT SAMMY WANTED TO TALK ABOUT

Of course, Sammy still wanted to complain about Owen 1. Sammy had been filled with excitement about learning about frogs, and now that was gone. I don't know why I said this, probably because I was mad, because really, it was not true. But I said it anyway: I said, "Owen 1 isn't so bad. I kind of like him." And that totally surprised Sammy.

WHAT HAPPENED NEXT

Sometimes when something unexpected happens and you are surprised by it, your brain suddenly stops working and then you can't think of a single thing to say. This is what happened to Sammy, and it lasted all the way to school.

WHAT HAPPENED AT SCHOOL

Sammy and I were almost late, so we went straight to our seats instead of hanging our stuff up in our lockers like usual. Mimi smiled at me but I did not smile back. I was still mad at her for leaving without me. Mimi looked at Sammy and Sammy waved at Mimi. Sammy is not a boy who understands body language. He was for sure not understanding that Mimi was saying, "What's wrong with Grace?"

MISS LOIS IS A TEACHER WHO DOES HER HOMEWORK

Just like she promised, Miss Lois had looked up the foods of the Dominican Republic. I was in a bad mood, but I still wanted to know what kind of things Mr. Frank was eating.

Miss Lois said that Mr. Frank was lucky to be trying so many new foods. These are the kinds of things she said he was probably eating.

BREAKFAST

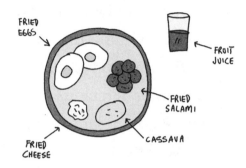

FRIED EGGS

FRUIT JUICE

FRIED SALAMI

FRIED CHEESE

CASSAVA

LUNCH

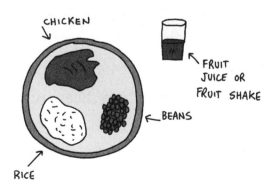

CHICKEN

FRUIT JUICE OR FRUIT SHAKE

BEANS

RICE

DINNER

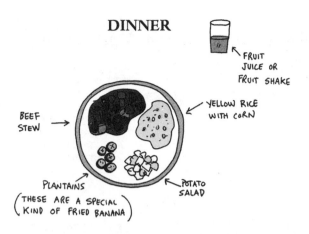

FRUIT JUICE OR FRUIT SHAKE

BEEF STEW →

YELLOW RICE WITH CORN

PLANTAINS
(THESE ARE A SPECIAL KIND OF FRIED BANANA)

POTATO SALAD

Miss Lois said cassava is a root and that you have to peel and then boil or soak it before you can eat it. You have to do this because it has a little bit of a poison called cyanide in it. But if you do these other things first, before you eat it, then it is safe. She said the boiling and the soaking part gets rid of the poison. Some of the boys were impressed that Mr. Frank was eating dangerous foods. I guess they were imagining every time he ate, he was in a scary movie. Maybe something like *Attack of the Root Vegetable.* Boys are so silly.

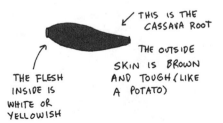

WHAT HAPPENED THAT WAS A SURPRISE

Miss Lois was talking some more about the Dominican Republic and we were all trying to pay attention when Owen 1 started kicking his desk. This always annoys me and makes me grumpy. I was already in the bad mood from before, so maybe that is why I turned around and hissed at Owen to *just stop it!* Owen 1 did not swallow his words. He looked straight at me and said, "Stop what?" Then he kicked his desk even faster, so now instead of *thump, thump, thump* it was *thump-thump, thump-thump, thump-thump.*

That's when I threw my pencil at him.

Sometimes you can totally surprise yourself by doing something you never thought in a million years you would do. This was one of those times!

THE LIST OF WHO SAW WHAT HAPPENED

Owen 1 (You don't get a pencil thrown at you and not notice it.)

Mimi (She looked even more surprised than me.)

Sammy

Owen 2

Grace F.

Ruth

Robert Walters

Miss Lois was not on the list, and for that I was super lucky.

HOW GRAVITY WORKS

If a pencil gets thrown in the air it will always fall back to the ground. Pencils cannot fly.

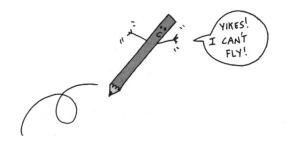

HOW A FALLING PENCIL CAN BE QUIET

If someone catches the pencil, then there will be no noise, because it will not hit a desk and it will not clatter around on the floor.

Owen 1 did not catch the pencil.

WHAT MISS LOIS SAID

Of course Miss Lois heard the pencil drop. She has supersonic ears, and even if she didn't, she would have heard it anyway because it made a lot of noise. Miss Lois looked right at Owen 1 and said, "Owen 1, stop fooling around. Pick up your pencil. One more outburst from you and you will be visiting Mr. Harris. Do you understand? And that means kicking the desk too."

I couldn't breathe. I was waiting for Owen 1 to say it. I was waiting for Owen 1 to point at me and say, "It wasn't me. It was Just Grace! She threw her pencil at me." I waited, and waited, and waited, but he didn't say anything. I had my eyes squeezed shut, because somehow when you are 100 percent sure something bad is about to happen, that is what your body wants to do. And then with my brain in the dark, I heard Miss Lois start talking about the Dominican Republic again.

WHAT MISS LOIS IS NOT

1 Miss Lois is not a detective.

If she were a detective she would have noticed that the pencil on the floor did not look like it had been chewed by a beaver, and because of that it could not have been a pencil belonging to Owen 1. Then she would have started an investigation about why there was a pencil on the ground, and for sure I would have gotten into trouble.

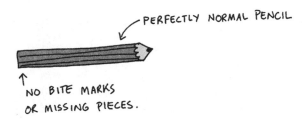

PERFECTLY NORMAL PENCIL

NO BITE MARKS OR MISSING PIECES.

2 Miss Lois is not a person with eyes in the back of her head.

If she were she would have seen that when I opened my eyes I turned around and looked right at Owen 1. And since he was smiling at me, I had to at least give him a thank-you smile back. Miss Lois did not see this because she only has eyes like a regular person, and she was drawing pictures of food on the front chalkboard.

3 Miss Lois is not a mind reader.

If she were a mind reader she would have known that at least seven people in her class were thinking about what had just happened and were not at all paying attention to what kids in the Dominican Republic eat for lunch.

THINGS I HAVE NEVER DONE AT SCHOOL

I am not a troublemaking girl. I do not take other people's things. I do not talk back to teachers. I do not lie about my homework. I do not pick on people. I do not tease people. I do not cheat on tests. I do not hit people, and before today, I did not throw things at people.

When you do something that you have never done before and it's a bad thing, it is really hard to believe that you actually did that thing. Your brain has a hard time getting used to the idea. Inside your head you say, *Did I really throw a pencil at Owen 1?* And then you answer, *Yes, I really did.* And you do this over and over about a million times, and then at the end, you finally have to believe it is true.

WHAT I WAS GLAD ABOUT (PART ONE)

I was glad that Sandra Orr was talking to Miss Lois about her project. Miss Lois finally said that she could do her project about foods from long ago. I think mostly she was tired of

Sandra Orr asking her about it every fifteen minutes. Sandra Orr loves princesses, and fairies, and all that castle kind of stuff. She especially loves unicorns, but we were not doing our projects about what animals ate, so I'm sure she was sad about that. Once Sandra Orr starts talking it is hard to get her to stop, so that meant I had lots of time to think my own thoughts and did not have to worry so much about paying attention.

WHAT I WAS GLAD ABOUT (PART TWO)

1 That my pencil did not hit Owen 1 in the eye, or even touch any part of his body. It's a good thing I am bad at aiming, because when I threw it, I was looking right at his nose.

2 That Owen 1 did not tell on me, though why he didn't is a big mystery.

3 That Marta did not see me throw the pencil, because she is the kind of girl that would have for sure told on me.

WHAT I AM EMBARRASSED ABOUT

That now I am the kind of girl who throws pencils at people. Even if only seven people know about it now, it will not stay that way.

By the time lunchtime is over, everyone will know.

HOW I FEEL

I wonder if this is how Owen 1 feels every time he does something wrong. This is not a good feeling to have. It is the kind of feeling that makes your stomach not hungry for lunch. It is the kind of feeling that makes you wish you had stayed at home. It's the kind of feeling that makes you want to disappear. It is the kind of feeling that makes you want to run and hide in the bathroom until lunch is over. It is the kind of feeling that makes you think that the bathroom idea is a really good plan.

THE ONLY GOOD THING

It was good that I had a stomachache, because if I was hungry, having to eat my lunch while hiding in the bathroom would be really disgusting.

WHAT WAS KIND OF SURPRISING

If you are just sitting in the bathroom doing nothing, you start to notice things. Things like who does and does not wash their hands after using the toilet.

CLEAN HAND   GERM-FILLED HAND

I am glad that I am not friends with Olivia Berchelli, because she did not wash her hands and for sure she was going back out to the lunchroom to finish her lunch.

WHAT MIMI SAID

Mimi found me hiding in the bathroom. She said I was not hard to find. She saw me go in, and then because I never came out, she knew I was still in there. It felt kind of dumb to be talking to her through the bathroom door, so I came out and we stood beside the sinks. I really couldn't think of what to say. What can you say when you do something crazy and you don't even know why you did it?

Finally Mimi said, "Let's not talk about it," and that was the perfect thing to say. Not talking about it and standing together felt almost like normal. Then Mimi said, "Let's get out of the bathroom," and that was a good idea too.

WHAT SAMMY STRINGER SAID

Sammy was not part of Mimi's let's-not-talk-about-it-and-make-Grace-feel-better plan, because as soon as we came out of the bathroom he said, "Wow, why did you do that?" He could have been talking about me hiding in the bathroom, but I was more sure that he was talking about the throwing-the-pencil thing. There are many parts that go together with doing something dumb. If this was how Owen 1 usually felt, I was wondering how he could stand it.

WHAT HAPPENS WHEN YOU DO SOMETHING DUMB

1 You do the dumb thing.

2 Usually you get in trouble for the dumb thing (but that didn't happen to me, at least not yet).

3 Everyone talks about you doing the dumb thing.

4 People ask you why you did the dumb thing.

5 People tell you that you should not have done the dumb thing.

6 People start to think of you as a dumb-thing-doer.

7 Other dumb-thing-doers (Owen 1) might now think that you are going to be their friend and that maybe now you will want to do dumb things together.

WHAT MIMI MADE ME THAT HELPED ME FEEL BETTER

A POTATO CHIP MAN MADE OUT OF A FEDEX ENVELOPE

WHAT MIMI SAID THAT WAS SUPPOSED TO MAKE ME FEEL BETTER

Mimi said that I was the best friend ever, and that for letting my dad help her with her hot dog project she had made me Mr. Potato Chip, and that the reason she did not wait for me to walk to school today was that she left early on purpose, so she could hide him in my locker for me to find. And then she took a big breath, because that was a lot to say all at once without breathing. I told Mimi a white lie — I had to. I said, "Oh, Mimi, I feel so, so, so much better," but really, the truth was, I was feeling about 98 percent guilty about how I had been secretly mad at her. Which means I was feeling maybe even worse than before, but now in a completely different way.

MR. POTATO CHIP

Mr. Potato Chip was pretty cool. It was nice to have a present, but it was even nicer to have something to talk about that was not about me. Mimi is super creative — she sewed him out of a plastic FedEx envelope.

She said she begged her mom to take her to the fabric store, but her mom said no, she was too busy. Finally, after looking around forever, she found the envelope and decided

to try sewing it. Mimi said she was excited to try to make other stuff out of the envelopes too, plus the extra-best part was that they were free. I promised to walk home with her so we could check out the FedEx box near the school for more supplies. It felt great to see her so excited and happy. From now on I was never going to let myself get jealous again.

WHAT HAPPENED IN THE AFTERNOON

Right away I could tell that everyone had been talking about me and my pencil throwing. During class there was lots of heads turning, and lots of watching of me and Owen 1. If you throw a pencil at someone, you should probably say you are sorry, even if that person is annoying and maybe deserved it at least a little bit. When Miss Lois was writing on the board I turned around and said, "Owen, I'm glad I didn't hit you with the pencil. I

shouldn't have, you know, thrown it at you."
I don't know what Owen thought about that
because I turned around real fast before he
could say anything. I probably should have
said something like "Thank you for not telling
on me," but now it was too late and I was not
going to be turning around again.

WHAT DOES NOT FEEL GOOD

It does not feel good to get poked in the back
with a pencil, even if it's not a super-sharp
pencil. Of course right away I knew it was
Owen 1, but I couldn't ignore him, so I had
to turn around. "Here's your pencil," he said.
I took it, but it did not look like my pencil
anymore. The end of it was all messed up
with bite marks. Yuck! I didn't want to be
touching it, but there was nothing else I could
do. "Thanks," I said, and it was a thank-you

meant for everything. It was a thank-you for the pencil, a thank-you for not saying anything to Miss Lois, and a thank-you for not trying to make me feel bad. It was a thank-you that made me suddenly feel a whole lot better. Still, after touching the pencil with Owen 1's bite marks on it, I was definitely going to have

to wash my hands. I was not going to be like Olivia Berchelli. I was going to use lots and lots of soap!

WHAT HAPPENED ON THE SCHOOL STEPS

Before Mimi and I had even taken five steps out of school, Jordan came running over and said, "Is it true? Did you punch Owen 1?" She seemed a little disappointed when I said no. "She threw a pencil at him," said Sammy. Sammy was being very sneaky lately, always creeping up behind me when I didn't even know he was there. "Did it hit him?" asked Jordan. I shook my head no again. "So it was nothing? Nothing happened?" "Yeah, nothing happened," I said, and then just saying that made it seem a whole ton better. Jordan was maybe disappointed, but I was not.

WALKING HOME WITH MIMI AND SAMMY

Of course Sammy wanted to know why Mimi and I were looking for FedEx supplies. He could not believe that Mimi had made Mr. Potato Chip all by herself — that's how good it looked. Sammy put a FedEx envelope on his head like a hat and wore it all the way to Max's house. He was dropping off Max's homework again so Max could catch up with his schoolwork and not miss out on stuff. It doesn't seem fair that even when you are sick you still have to do homework.

After Sammy left, Mimi asked me if I was feeling okay about everything. I gave her one of my looks that means, *Yeah, I'm okay.* She knows me and she knows my looks, so she said, "Good, I was worried." Mimi said she was going to go home and try to make a stuffed hot dog out of FedEx envelopes so she could use it for her project. She is so creative!

WHO WAS OUTSIDE

Augustine Dupre was in the side yard doing some planting work. She was happy to see me. "Look, I bought some catnip for Crinkles. Do you think he will like it?" Cats love catnip so I said I was pretty sure he would. Not that Augustine Dupre needed to be planting things to make Crinkles love her more. That cat thinks she is the best thing ever. If he were a person, they would be in love and married for sure.

I told Augustine Dupre all about my bad day. While I was telling her the story, she did lots of sighing. French people like to do that kind of thing. It means either they are tired and bored with you, or they are feeling sorry for you. Augustine Dupre was definitely feeling sorrow for me, I could tell.

Then Augustine Dupre said something that was totally strange and unexpected. She said that it seemed like Owen 1 was a little bit lucky for me. First his bad actions with Sunni turned into something good for me, the not having to study the insides of frogs. Then when I did something bad, his actions, not telling on me, also turned out good for me. Of course I would never in a million years have thought to think of it that way, but that's how Augustine Dupre is. She is always looking at things in different and interesting ways. She changed yucky into lucky.

WHAT I WAS THINKING NEXT

After my talk with Augustine Dupre, my head was not as much mixed up. Now suddenly what I had said to Sammy just to make him quiet might actually be a little bit true. I did not like Owen 1 very much better, but now I was thinking that under all his annoyingness and troublemaking outsides, he might sometimes be okay. That's kind of an important thing to know. It's the difference between all good and all bad.

It was maybe the reason why Miss Lois always seems to be trying to give Owen 1 chances to do better. She thinks he's only trouble on the outside. She could be sending him to see the principal every twenty minutes, but instead lets him stay in class and tries to get him to pay attention. She is probably hoping she can change him. I don't know if she's going to be a success: Owen 1 is a ton of work. People like Sunni are easier. They are already perfect. They came that way.

WHAT I AM GOING TO MAKE FOR MIMI

I for sure wanted to be an all-good friend for Mimi, just like she was an all-good friend for me, so I had a great idea to make a zine for her about hot dogs. I didn't have to do any research because I have heard Dad talk about hot dogs forever, so I already know all about the things I am going to draw.

I was just starting when Mom called me down for dinner.

WHAT WAS UNUSUAL ABOUT DINNER

Dad was not at dinner, which was too bad because I was really wanting to ask him about his big plan for Friday and why we were not going to get to go out for dinner anymore.

Mom was no help in telling me "the secret." It's too bad for me, but she is maybe the best secret keeper in the whole world. She never tells secrets ever. She could have a brain full of important stuff and no one would ever know. If she hadn't married Dad, she could have been a fantastic secret agent.

Mom said that since we were staying home on Friday, I could invite a few more of my friends for dinner. Even when I said that it was going to be impossible to get people to come to a mystery dinner, she still wouldn't tell me what the surprise was. She is good.

ZINETASTIC

After dinner I went back upstairs to finish working on Mimi's zine. My favorite part is when you are all finished with the drawing, and then you get to fold it up into a little book.

I just kept looking at it over and over again. I loved it. I wonder if this is how Mimi feels when she is finished making a stuffed animal. It probably is, because it is a feeling that makes you want to do another one right away. I have zine fever.

COVER OF MIMI'S ZINE

WHAT I SAW RIGHT BEFORE BED

I was happy to see Mimi in her window, looking at me, right before I went to bed. I held up the zine and pointed to it even though I knew that she could not tell what it was. When you are excited about something you have to show it off, no matter what. She held up Willoughby and then I held up Chip-Up, and that meant we were both going to bed happy.

WHAT I DO NOT WANT FOR BREAKFAST

Today I do not want French toast for breakfast. Today I do not want to save the world. Today I want to be ordinary, nothing special, not spectacular. Today I want to be boring.

TASTY
LITTLE
O's

WALKING TO SCHOOL

Mimi was waiting for me, and I was 100 percent glad about that. I could not wait to give her the hot dog zine. She loved it, and she especially loved that it was like a little book. That was my favorite part too. She said it would be cool to have a whole bunch of them about all sorts of different things, which is exactly what I was thinking. "You could make one about Mr. Potato Chip." Mimi is so full of good ideas.

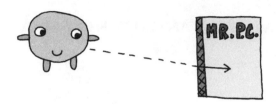

We met up with Sammy and Max about halfway to school. Max said he was feeling a lot better, which was good news because I did not want to get sick just by walking with him. This kind of thing can happen if you are still contagious, but he said he was fine and not to worry. I told them all about the mystery dinner, and both Max and Sammy said they wanted to come, even though I had not even 1 percent of an idea about what we were going to be eating.

WHAT HAPPENED LIKE USUAL

Miss Lois talked.

Owen 1 banged his foot on his desk.

I did not throw a pencil.

I did not feel like throwing a pencil.

Owen 1 asked to go to the bathroom about twelve times.

WHAT THIS MEANS (PART ONE)

I am not a troublemaking girl. I am me. Like normal. I am cured.

WHAT THIS MEANS (PART TWO)

Owen 1 is still a troublemaking boy. Owen 1 is still Owen 1. Like normal. Owen 1 is not cured.

Miss Lois still has a lot more work to do to help fix him.

WHAT HAPPENED AT SCHOOL THAT WAS EXCITING

For the whole day, nothing, and that was exactly how I was hoping it was going to turn out to be.

WHAT I THOUGHT ABOUT DOING

I was thinking about inviting Grace F. to the mystery dinner.

This was not as easy as it sounds at first. If I invited only Grace F., then I would feel guilty about not inviting the other two Graces. If all the Graces came, then I would have to be with them as well as with Mimi, and then Mimi, who is my most important friend ever, might not feel so special. This is not a chance I was wanting to take, so I

didn't invite Grace F. or anyone else. It was
easier that way.

**DIAGRAM OF THE BEST WAY
FOR IT TO WORK**

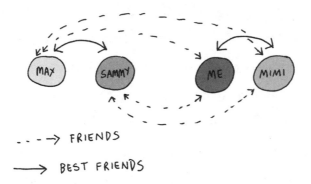

----> FRIENDS

——> BEST FRIENDS

WE ARE DIFFERENT

Max, Sammy, and Mimi were not filled with
wondering about the mystery dinner like I
was. They didn't even really want to talk about
it. We were different, because I couldn't wait
to get home to ask Dad what it was all going
to be about.

WHAT HAPPENED

Dad said, "It's a surprise. I can't tell you." I said, "Come on, Dad, please? Please tell me! I'm dying!" Dad said, "Are you sure you want to know? It'll ruin the surprise. Aren't surprises more fun?" And then I thought about birthday presents and Christmas presents and how I always said I wanted to know what was inside them right away, but really if I thought about it, I kind of liked the not-knowing and the waiting part, because it made everything more exciting. So I said, "Okay, you can surprise me." And then Dad was happy and

 smiling, but I was still filled with wondering and not knowing, and it did not feel one bit like Christmas.

WHAT I SAID NEXT

"Dad, can you give me one little hint about it, just one word or two words? I won't ask anything else. I promise." "Potato chip," said Dad, and I almost fell over in surprise.

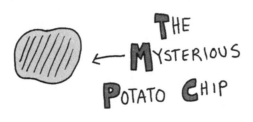

THE MYSTERIOUS POTATO CHIP

THE THING ABOUT SURPRISES

I don't know how she is so smart about the world, but I think Augustine Dupre is right about how it can take forever to know a person. I have known Dad for my whole entire life, and he can still surprise me. If I knew everything about him, the surprises part would not be possible.

THE THING ABOUT DAD

A lot of the time Dad does not seem like he is paying attention. The surprise part is that he is.

SOMETIMES

Sometimes I draw when I am sad, and sometimes I draw when I am happy. It's the one thing that always makes my whole body feel good even though my hand is the only part of my body that gets to move.

I CAN MAKE EVERYTHING OKAY.

WHAT I DID BEFORE BED

I flashed my lights and waved at Mimi's window even though she wasn't there. I wonder if she ever does that to me?

WALKING TO SCHOOL

Mimi and I walked to school together, just like always. We tried to think about what the potato chip surprise was, but we didn't have any excellent guesses. "Your dad is too tricky," said Mimi. And she was right.

WHAT IS HARD TO DO

It is hard to wait for a whole day of school to be over when you know that you are having a surprise waiting for you at home.

WHAT I DID NOT WANT TO HEAR

I did not want to listen to Miss Lois reminding us about our projects being due on Monday. I did not want to listen to Owen 1 tell the whole class his project was going to be the best ever.

I did not want to listen to Aurora Gambit tell us the list of weird ice cream flavors she had found out about, but Miss Lois said that she could, so now I know that there is ice cream that is flavored like sweet potatoes, rose petals, octopus, bacon, pepper, and mango with seaweed.

I did not want to listen to any of this because I wanted to go home.

When the bell finally rang, Owen 1 came over to me and said, "I'm doing my project about people who eat bugs." This was of course totally surprising to me because I was 100 percent thinking that Sammy was the one who was doing the bug-eating project. But Owen 1 did not even give me enough time to be surprised about that, because what he said next was even more surprising. "Guess what I'm bringing to the snack party? Chocolate-covered ants!" Then he just stood there looking very happy with himself waiting for me to say something. When you are surprised by something it's not always easy to think of what to say. Finally I just asked, "Are you going to eat the ants?" "No way," said Owen 1, "and I'm not going to tell anyone they're eating ants in the chocolate until the end." Then he smiled and left.

Owen 1 is a weird kid. Was he warning me about the ants so I wouldn't eat them, or was he bragging about them because he thought I was now in the troublemaking club like he was? Either way, I was 100 percent not going to be eating any ants on Monday, and for that I said another quiet-so-he-couldn't-hear-me thank-you.

LOOKS LIKE NORMAL CHOCOLATE WITH NORMAL EYES.

WHAT IT WOULD LOOK LIKE WITH X-RAY EYES.

WHAT MIMI TOLD ME

Right after class Mimi said that Jordan told her that Olivia told her that Owen 1 said that he heard I liked him. There was only one person in the whole world who would have said that to him, and that person was Sammy. You have to be careful about what you say to people, because words can get around. Normally I might have been kind of mad at Sammy for a thing like that, but today I wasn't. Suddenly I was 100 percent sure that Sammy saying that to Owen 1 was the reason I was not going to be eating any chocolate-covered ants on Monday. So then, right when I wasn't expecting it, it was time for another quiet thank-you.

MY HEAD WITH NORMAL EYES.

MY HEAD WITH X-RAY EYES.

IT IS FILLED WITH QUIET THANK-YOUS.

THANK YOU THANK YOU THANK YOU THANK YOU THANK

WHAT HAPPENED ON THE WAY HOME

I was so excited about going home that it made me not even care about Sammy being gossipy and people talking about me liking Owen 1. I didn't even feel like saying one thing to him about it either. I think my excited surprise-dinner feelings finally rubbed off on Mimi, Max, and Sammy too. Because by the time we got to my house we were almost running.

WHAT WAS IN THE DINING ROOM

Every bowl that Mom has in the whole house was on the dining room table. Each bowl had a number on it and every bowl was filled to the top with potato chips. I couldn't believe it. It was a potato chip buffet. Mom said Dad had been collecting different-flavored potato chips all week and now we were going to do some taste testing. Sometimes all you can think of to say is wow. We all said, "Wow." There was nothing else to say.

Mom said we should all grab some pens and paper and get eating to try to guess what the different flavors were. Even though there was a pad of paper for everyone, Sammy went to get a notebook from his backpack. I didn't think that was weird until I saw Sammy rubbing a chip in his notebook. Sometimes when someone is doing something strange, you just have to ask about it. With Sammy that's a good rule, because he is probably doing something you would never be able to guess in a million years.

Sammy said that he was keeping a diary of all the food he was eating. Every time he ate something he would rub the food on his paper and then write down what it was. It sounded a lot like what Sammy's shirts used to look like after he had finished lunch, except for the writing part. I didn't say that, though, because he was a guest at my house, so it was important to be polite.

SAMMY'S SHIRT

SAMMY'S JOURNAL

Once I got used to Sammy rubbing potato chips in his notebook it didn't bug me anymore — it almost seemed normal. That's how stuff works with Sammy. The more time you spend around him, the more you start thinking that weird stuff is just not that unusual.

The party was fantastic. It was the most amazing chip party ever! Everyone had different favorites, but we mostly all hated the same flavors.

Some of the favorites were salt and pepper, barbecue, sour cream and onion, salt and vinegar, ketchup, and artichoke and spinach.

There were a few that we kids didn't like. Island jerk, arrabiata, and sweet chili and red pepper were really spicy. Only Mom and Dad liked those ones. No one liked Chesapeake Bay beer chips, pesto and smoked mozzarella chips, or buffalo bleu chips. The blue cheese–flavored chips were not something I was ever going to like, but Mom is a big blue cheese fan so I was surprised that she didn't like them. The big disappointment for me was the garlic mashed flavor. I love mashed potatoes, but I did not love these chips. They did not taste like garlic mashed potatoes at all.

WHAT WAS SO FUN

The best part was trying to guess what all the different flavors were. It was a party for our tongues! If you eat a lot of potato chips you will not be very hungry for dinner. Mom and Dad had some interesting ideas about dinner too.

WHAT IS A CHIPWICH?

You take two slices of bread and put either mayonnaise (which I find disgusting) or butter on the bread. Then you put as many chips as you can on one of the slices. When that is done you put the other slice on top and push it down until all the chips are smooshed and crushed. Then you eat it. Mom said this is how she used to make her tuna salad sandwiches when she was a kid.

We all tried a chipwich with our favorite chips. For sure it would have been excellent with Augustine Dupre's French roast chicken chips, but I didn't mention that. Dad asked if we wanted to order pizzas, but really all we wanted to do was drink tons and tons of water. Chip eating makes you very, very thirsty!

MAKE YOUR OWN CHIPWICH

① BUTTER TWO SLICES OF BREAD.

②

PUT AS MANY CHIPS AS YOU CAN ON ONE OF THE SLICES.

③ PUT OTHER SLICE OF BREAD ON TOP.

④

SMASH CHIPS IN BETWEEN THE TWO SLICES.

THE WISH CHIP

I didn't know this, but there is a special chip called a wish chip. If you make a wish while you eat it, your wish is supposed to come true. It's kind of like the birthday wish with the blowing out of the candles. Dad said he used to look for wish chips every time he ate chips when he was little. He was explaining how it all worked and what kind of chips we should be looking for when Mimi said, "Is this one?" Lucky Mimi. She found the one and only wish chip at the whole party. Dad said she had to put the whole thing in her mouth and make a wish while she was crunching it up.

Mimi had her eyes closed for a long time like she was wishing for something really special or really important. Sammy asked what she wished for but she said she couldn't tell him or else the wish wouldn't come true. Everyone knows you can't talk about your wishes or they won't come true, but even still, you can't help wondering what someone is wishing for.

NORMAL CHIP

WISH CHIP

← CHIP IS FOLDED IN HALF.

MIMI'S WISH

Mimi wanted to tell me something about her wish. I could just tell. She was being just like Owen 1, trying to keep the words inside as hard as she could. But they weren't listening to her — they wanted to come out. I gave her my you-can-tell-me look. But she shook her head and said, "No, I can't." That made me want to know what she was thinking about even more. After I gave her my please-please-please-I-won't-tell-anyone look she said, "Okay, just a hint." Then Mimi said, "Sister." "Are you wishing for a sister?" I couldn't believe that. Mimi nodded yes, and that made me a little sad for her.

Wishing for a sister was like wishing for a magic carpet, a dog, or a million dollars — those kind of things didn't just all of a sudden happen. They were kind of on the impossible-probably-never-going-to-happen list. You couldn't just pick up a catalogue and order one. Poor Mimi. I didn't even know she wanted a sister. I gave her my it'll-be-okay look, but she didn't need it. She wasn't even sad. She was smiling.

IMAGINARY SISTER CATALOGUE

WHAT WE DID TO MAKE MOM FEEL GOOD

Mom was really worried about feeding everyone potato chips for dinner, so we all forced down some fruit salad to make her feel better. Parents are always nervous about healthy eating, so it was a surprise that she was even letting us have a chip party. When

things like this happen it really makes you happy with the parents you ended up with. I was feeling pretty lucky about Mom and Dad.

Sammy was happy about the fruit salad. I guess it's easier to make marks on paper with fruit than it is with chips. His chips page was pretty boring, but his fruit page was very colorful.

Max was happy about the fruit salad too. He is doing his report about foods you can eat on a stick. You can't eat potato chips on a stick, no matter how hard you try.

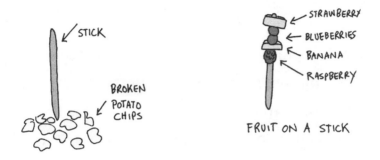

STICK

BROKEN
POTATO
CHIPS

STRAWBERRY
BLUEBERRIES
BANANA
RASPBERRY

FRUIT ON A STICK

WHAT COULD HAPPEN NEXT?

Mom said we could go out to dinner on Saturday if we still wanted to try something new. This was not a question I wanted to be asked right then. I don't know how she could even talk about food after eating so many chips, and chipwiches, and fruit salad. My stomach was screaming, "No more food!" and my brain was saying, "I don't even want to talk about it."

WHAT HAPPENED AFTER DINNER

Mimi, Sammy, Max, and I all watched two hours of *Unlikely Heroes* videos. The last one was about a man who saved three people from drowning when their plane crashed into the ocean. The man was for sure a hero, because he had saved the people all by himself. When he was on TV, he said it was hard for him to think happy thoughts about everything that had happened, because every time he thought about it, he just remembered how one of the people he was saving had almost drowned. "I almost lost him," said the hero man. Then he said he didn't like thinking about the plane accident at all, because it scared him to think of what might have happened if things had not turned out the way they had.

Sammy and Max said, "That's crazy. He's a hero." Mimi said she thought that the man should be happy about the people he had saved and try not to think about anything else. This seemed like a good idea, and mostly I bet the man wanted to do that, but it's not always easy to make your brain not think certain thoughts. Sometimes your brain just wants to wonder about certain things, and no matter what you do, you can't make it stop.

Things like . . .

Why *did* I throw that pencil?

Am I really an all-good person?

Is Owen 1 a troublemaker inside and out?

Will Miss Lois be able to save him?

Should I tell Mimi, Sammy, and Max about the chocolate ants?

Do I like or not like Owen 1?

WHAT DID HAPPEN NEXT

Of course I told Mimi, Sammy, and Max all about Owen 1's chocolates. Sammy and Max couldn't believe it. Mimi said she was not surprised that Owen 1 would try to play a sneaky trick on everyone. She said we definitely had to tell Miss Lois about it, and she was probably right about that. You couldn't just let people eat insects without them knowing about it. Owen 1 was for sure going to be mad at me for telling, but that was probably better than having the whole entire class mad at me for not telling. It's not always easy to do the right thing.

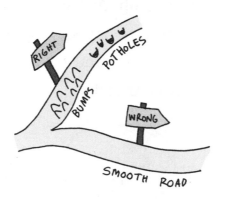

Even though nothing had happened yet, I knew exactly how it was going to work out. Owen 1 was going to be sad about the ants, and when that happened my empathy power was going to start working. I was going to feel guilty about telling on him, so to make up for it I was going to work extra hard to be nice to him. He would feel my nice friendly energy and then, of course, he would think that it was true that I liked him. In the end it was going to be just like what had happened with Sammy all over again. And even though my brain didn't want it to happen, my heart was going to win. Owen 1 and I were probably going to sort of be friends.

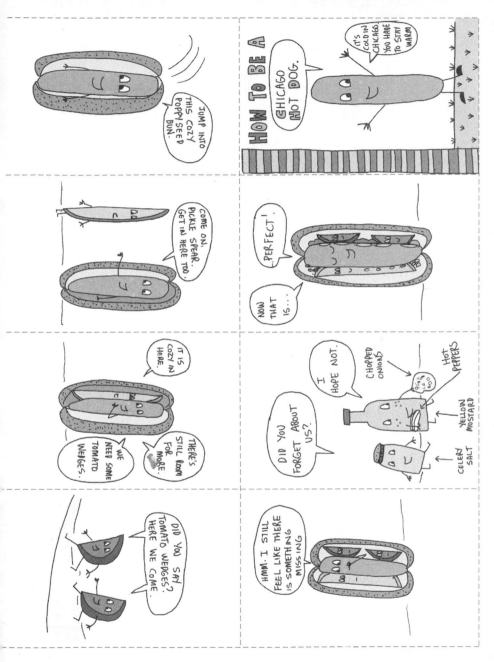

To make this zine see instructions on pages 44 to 46.